ILARIE VORONCA

THE CONFESSION
OF A FALSE SOUL

TRANSLATED BY
SUE BOSWELL

AND WITH AN INTRODUCTION BY
BRENDAN CONNELL

THIS IS A SNUGGLY BOOK

ISBN: 978-1-64525-066-1

"ILARIE VORONCA" was the pen name of Eduard Marcus (1903-1946), one of the greatest avant-garde writers of his time. A Jewish Romanian by birth, he published numerous texts in his home country before permanently establishing himself in France, where he produced volumes of poetry and prose in the French language, including *L'Apprenti fantôme et Cinq poèmes de septembre* (1938), *La Clé des réalités* (1944), and *Souvenir de la planète Terre* (1945).

SUE BOSWELL studied French Language and Literature at UCL and for a time taught French at Goldsmiths University of London. She then moved into university administration, specialising in university external relations and communications. Later she became a translator for the Wiener Holocaust Library. Her translations include *The Assassins and other Stories* by Marcel Schwob and *The Last Train* by Arnaud Rykner (both Snuggly Books 2020). Sue lives with her husband, Colin Boswell, in London and Ouveillan, a village near Narbonne in the Languedoc.

BRENDAN CONNELL has published numerous works of fiction and translations. The former include *Unpleasant Tales* (Eibonvale Press, 2013). His translations include Guido Gozzano's *Alcina and Other Stories* (Snuggly Books, 2019).

CONTENTS

INTRODUCTION

Eduard Marcus, who wrote under the pen name of "Ilarie Voronca," was born into a Jewish family on the 31st of December, 1903, in the eastern Romanian town of Brăila, and died by suicide on the 8th of April, 1946, in Paris.

Voronca's early poems, symbolist in tone, were published in the avant-garde magazine *Sburătorul*, in 1922. Under the influence of a modernist manifesto published in *Contimporanul*, another Romanian avant-garde magazine, however, he quickly changed his style and, in 1924, together with his like-minded friends Victor Brauner and Stephan Roll, published a single-issue review called *75 HP* which, with its striking red and black format, was remarkable for the typographical and graphic audacity it displayed.

Upon receiving his law degree in 1925, Voronca moved to Paris, where he was hired by the Abeille insurance company, and two years later, in 1927, published *Colomba*, a volume of poetry, named after his wife, which was his first clear venture into surrealism. In 1928 another book of poetry, *Ulise*, was released, which contained an illustration by Marc Chagall showing the author as the Eiffel Tower, and then in 1929 *Plante si animale*, with illustrations by Constantin Brancusi. All three of these books were published in Romanian by the Imprimerie Union, a press established in Paris by Volf Chalit and Dimitri Snégaroff, two Russian Jews whose publishing venture was geared towards the Eastern European immigrant community in France.

In 1929 Voronca returned to Romania, where he lived and published for the next four years, before establishing himself permanently in France, in 1933. The following year saw the publication of *Poèmes parmi les hommes*, the first of his books to be written in French, the language in which, from this point forward, all his books were written. In all, during his lifetime, he   published seventeen books in French—volumes of poetry, short stories, and novels.

La Confession d'une âme fausse, which, expertly translated in the present volume under the title *The Confession of a False Soul*, was Voronca's second novel, appearing in 1942, a year after *Lord Duveen ou L'invisible à la portée de tous*, in the midst of the second world war, released by Méridien, a small publishing house specialising in avant-garde works. Considering the date of the book, and the fact that the "soul" that the central character ends up with is one of a dead soldier, one might be tempted to call the book a war novel—but such a definition, while in part true, would oversimplify a work which, though written in the simplest of styles, is psychologically quite complex.

During the time of the short novel's composition, the author was living in Marseille, and was engaged in activities with the French resistance. As a Jew he was certainly as aware as anyone of the situation in Europe and the implications of the Nazis ruling France. Yet, in the novel, none of this is directly addressed. Aside from a séance, in which we hear directly from the "false soul," life seems to be running a normal course. There are fairs, dinners among friends, outdoor cafés at which people sit. But all this is seen as if in a dream; and thus the book is a wonderful exemplar of the surreal. The arcs and curves of what might be called "story telling" are reduced to cubist refractions.

Voronca's brand of surrealism is much softer than that of most of his fellow-travelers, but it is also considerably more sympathetic, in large part because it is also considerably less self-indulgent. His chronicles, though as full of magic as those of his literary colleagues, are also more public. The themes, though not always universal, are not those which repel or uninvite. *The Confession of a False Soul* is, after all, a novel of searching and, in its own way, of love—motifs that few cannot relate to.

The English-speaking world has paid little attention to the work of Ilarie Voronca, especially his prose, but it is hoped that the present volume will help remedy that situation, for he was a highly gifted author of unique vision whose writing is certainly deserving, not only of a marked position in the surrealist canon, but also one in the lists of great European literature.

—Brendan Connell

ILARIE VORONCA

THE CONFESSION
OF A FALSE SOUL

TRANSLATED BY
SUE BOSWELL

AND WITH AN INTRODUCTION BY
BRENDAN CONNELL

I

A STRANGE SURGEON

It was a strange surgeon who removed your soul in the twinkling of an eye.

"It won't hurt," he was saying, "lean back in this armchair."

And he talked to you about this and that. About the return of the fine weather, about the latest production at the opera house, about the secret peace talks. For we were of course at war. And there was a constant threat of peace. So your spirit wandered, now around the battlefield, now around the noisy city streets. And just when you were least expecting it this clever character wrenched your soul from you.

"You see," he was saying with a smile, "it didn't kill you. It's done."

And he showed you, gripped between small pincers, a white thing with blood dripping from it.

For myself, I felt dizzy. And I made for the door, feeling my way.

"Rest a little before you go," said the soul-remover again. And already he was forgetting me, he was attending to other clients, inviting one of them into his office.

The waiting room was full of people, some leafing through magazines, others talking amongst themselves with the mysterious air of conspirators.

"Didn't it hurt a lot?" I was asked by a gentleman with dyed hair, hiding his no doubt advanced age behind a juvenile appearance.

He must have interrupted a story which was close to his heart, for without waiting for my answer he turned towards his neighbours and continued:

"Yes, she had the cheek to claim the umbrella belonged to her. I myself recognised it straight away. My aunt who had hired her on my recommendation, for she had worked as a cleaner for me, was watching us without saying anything. I took the umbrella and asked her:

"'If it's yours, where did you buy it?'

"'Here in Nice,' she replied.

"Then I opened the umbrella, holding it over my head.

"'Look,' I said to her, and she read on the inside label: 'Camboulives, rue des Marchands, Avignon'.

"It was in Avignon that I'd bought it. Camboulives had a shop—this was before the previous peace (for at that time you counted time passing by the peace accords which shared it), at the corner of the rue des Marchands and the rue Neuve.

"'You're nothing but a thief.'

"Do you believe she dared reply? She kept quiet. It was she who also stole my sugar, and my jam . . ."

17

Now the door opened. The client coming out was staggering and he came and collapsed next to me. He was suffering from a great fright. His whole body was shaking.

"Did he take yours too?" I couldn't help asking him.

"No," he replied. "My soul has had a split in it for a while. Life was difficult . . . I was losing myself. So I came to see the surgeon. He's going to do a repair for me. To start with he has to enlarge the hole to get to my soul. The next time he'll seal it."

I was already feeling better. But I was still feeling a great emptiness. I was like a house with its doors and windows broken, with the wind blowing around everywhere inside me.

The man whose soul was going to be sealed watched me for a few moments as if to make a better judgement on how I looked and said to me:

"Why don't you get an artificial soul made? A golden one, that's rather expensive," he added quickly, for I had started to look embarrassed, "but you could order one made out of something more reasonable, rubber for example."

With permission from those who were waiting I went back into the surgeon's office. My words did not come easily, for the wound was still fresh and, in addition, words made to measure for my soul were now floating aimlessly around the empty space inside me.

"What you are asking for," replied the surgeon, "can be done and I can even arrange a payment schedule. Thank God, we're still at war, and the souls of robust men are in plentiful supply. Yours could no longer be saved. To keep it would have exposed you to serious suffering, later, when removing it would no longer have been possible. Weighted down with pus, that soul would have dragged you with it into the depths of a real hell. But science has progressed, and as I said to you, we are at war. As long as those troublemakers who're threatening us with peace don't succeed we can rest easy. We get an excellent crop of souls every day. As you can well imagine, it would be a shame to leave souls, most of which are in perfect condition, on the corpses of the battlefield. Of course, the preparatory work required takes quite a time; the souls have to be treated and adapted on assembly mounts. The best mounts are the gold ones, but they also make them of rubber. That's what yours will be made of. It will last you easily five or six years. Then it might have to be repaired. But first let's wait until your wound heals over."

Despite the easy payment schedule my earnings as an assistant filing clerk in a Finance Company were well below the price I had to pay. So I went back to the surgeon.

"Wouldn't there be some way to provide me with a cheaper soul?" I asked him. "Since you reassured me that unless the person with the false soul is very careless that soul is not noticeable, I would be content with one from an animal, for example."

"Don't even think of it!" cried the surgeon. "Don't you know that animals have almost completely disappeared? It's true that we men of science had managed to extract some very hard-wearing souls from them which suited quite a few humans very well. Fixed to very expensive mounts (although one could at a pinch make do with more ordinary ones) these souls were the most sought after. I've known some highly placed people with the souls of pigs. Some great scholars had resorted to the souls of donkeys. And they were very happy with them. Look at these," the surgeon added, showing me a huge card index. "These contain the names of famous clients for whom I adapted the souls of bullocks, dogs, cats. I've even experimented with rats' souls (amongst my clients are some financiers fitted with those) but they have a tendency towards melancholia and a persecution mania which makes their use very hit and miss. We don't need rats at this time. That goes back a long way. Earth was plentiful and there were excellent animals all around us. Their souls were all happy and optimistic. Rats, owls, bats, melancholic and tough crows were to be avoided. Would you have suspected that economists and statisticians would have passed through my office to get themselves provided with the souls of geese and parrots? You must admit that the work was impeccable. Alas, bullocks, horses, donkeys, cows, pigs, geese, dogs and cats have all become too rare now. In place of animals we have machines—the glories of our technology—tanks, aeroplanes, submarines, and we can be justly proud of them, but we must admit it: these machines do not have flesh to satisfy our hunger, nor souls to replace our sick and ruined ones. Yet, who knows?" the surgeon added thoughtfully. "We need to think about this. Perhaps these machines do have souls? And then we could extract them for the benefit of humans. Why not adapt a railway engine's soul for an engineer, a ship's soul for a sailor, a dynamo's soul for an electrician? All that is still in the realm of dreams and years of laboratory research. For you, it will be a soldier's soul."

II

A FALSE SOUL

A few days later I was leaving the surgeon's office armed with the fine apparatus of a false soul.

"At the beginning, take care," the surgeon instructed me as I left him, "don't wear it all the time, let your body get used to it gradually. Don't make too much noise, don't laugh too loudly, because people might notice that your soul is false. In the end, I think you'll be pleased."

He hadn't said anything to me about the life of the man whose soul he had given me. Before letting me leave with it, he had subjected me to several fittings. Nevertheless, for the moment it was bothering me a great deal. Deep in my breast was a heaviness. I stopped in front of a mirror and looked curiously at myself. My eyes were fairly clear, my face showed obvious satisfaction. Ha! Good! I wasn't too bad, and anyone seeing me would have been taken with my shining soul. My soul! Ha! My God, above all I mustn't let anyone see that it was just a prosthesis.

It took only a few days for it to settle properly inside me. I walked about proudly and elegantly. Oh! What a noble and distinguished soul, people would say when they saw me. And I hid as best I could the fact that this soul had belonged to a soldier who had died somewhere at the front. Who knows, perhaps it was the soul of handsome and brave officer. Maybe a general. No! Certainly not. The noble souls of such personages must be reserved for wealthier clients. This one must rather have been the soul of a poor bugler, a low ranker. What does it matter? It was a valiant and healthy soul. The souls of civilians dying in their beds of sickness or old age were wrinkled, dried up, unusable. But soldiers, as the surgeon had said to me, died young, healthy and joyful, at the height of their strength and glory. So their souls were perfect for use. Mine turned out to be infinitely superior to the one that had been removed from me. Obviously, I felt a tightening of my heart strings when a charming young lady I was courting said, "How could I not love you when you have such a beautiful soul. For even if you're not handsome or clever, I shall always love you for your beautiful soul . . ." I would feel ashamed then, and was afraid that the blush rising to my brow would give away my deception. I was a little reassured by the fact that on several occasions I had recognised postures and attitudes on the part of famous people who were adored by women and the multitudes, which gave away the fact that they too were wearing prosthetic souls. I was perhaps the only person to notice, for I myself had adopted the same attitudes as them to try my best to hide the false nature of my soul. After all, I would say to myself, why not take advantage? The woman I fancy won't notice. Nor the men amongst whom I display my brilliance.

I quickly realised also that a number of problems linked to my old soul had now disappeared. The regrets, anxieties, torments were far away. I was unaffected by setbacks that came my way. Nothing hurt me. I no longer had any scruples. I looked in the best of health.

Clearly, the soul they had adapted for me must have undergone a previous treatment in order to resist heat and cold, disappointments and even injustices. At night I slept, with no suffering and no dreams. I no longer had that vague sadness which often assailed my real soul. In those days I would have to pay for the slightest joy with suffering. I had been like a dog which has to bite into the bone of sadness to find the marrow of pleasure. Now, indifferent to pain, everything had become for me a reason for delight. Why hadn't I realised earlier?

I could have had my soul removed at a young age in order to have one mounted on rubber. Of course, there were disadvantages too. When the weather was too hot it would weigh down on me quite heavily. Also, eventually, it had nibbled away a little at the inside of my body. I had some small sores at the corners of my lips. But those were small inconveniences compared with the advantages I was getting. And, in the end, why argue about it, my own soul—as the soul-remover had told me—was too damaged. I should consider myself lucky to have been able to get myself a false one.

III

THE SPIRITUALIST'S SÉANCE

One evening, however, I had a real fright. I was at the house of a friend who had planned a surprise for me, to join in a spiritualist's séance. I'm fairly sceptical of these sorts of displays, so had always avoided participating. But that evening I had not been forewarned. And even if I had been, I might have gone, for I didn't think I had anything to be afraid of.

So there we were gathered around a table. The lights had been turned out. I was trying not to laugh when I heard the lady of the house announce in a serious voice that the spirit had entered the room.

"Speak," she said to it, "speak, spirit, we're listening."

How ridiculous that all seemed to me.

But suddenly a voice sounding like mine and coming more or less from my mouth began to speak:

"For the short period of time that I spent on this earth," said the voice, "I was a soldier. From a very young age I was trained in the harsh profession of the military. At school I learned about the trajectory of bullets, I calculated the range of artillery, the firepower of aeroplanes and ships. From the age of eighteen I took part in battles, I was a machine gunner. Sometimes, as I hid in a bush waiting for the enemy, a vision would come from far away, from a forgotten ancestor, to haunt my soul. I saw myself working with the glorious tools of my trade. I was finishing polishing a table, or a door. I was a joiner or carpenter. And in the evening, when I left the workshop which smelled of sweet wood and resin, I would go for a walk in the communal gardens. Snatches of fanfares, with their mixed militant and romantic echoes which I was amazed to hear, breathed into my ears. The life I was leading was certainly adventurous and free, but I felt that calm, that joy, were elsewhere. One day a bullet went through my chest. I thought everything was over, for ever. They took my corpse behind the lines. Nurses leaned over me, they injected me, they applied leeches, they pierced me with syringes to extract my soul which had been numbed by my fatal injury. Then, in a surgeon's office . . ."

"Enough!" I shouted then, and, getting up quickly, I turned on the lights. Another second and the mischievous soldier would have spoken my name. I did my best to calm the protests of the lady of the house who was regretting that such a loquacious spirit had been prevented from finishing his confession. I took leave of my friends and swore to myself to avoid all such gatherings in future. Think what a disaster if my soul had been shown to be a transplanted one.

For a time I remained constantly on the alert. I would turn down invitations from friends and went from my workplace to my bedroom where I shut myself in alone. The surgeon had not warned me that in certain circumstances the false soul was able to speak. I had discovered that the shadows and vapours of a spiritualist séance were amongst these circumstances. But there were perhaps others, where the spirit inhabiting me would recover the power of speech. So for now, I distrusted everything.

However, a few days later I had forgotten the unfortunate happening, and I started going outside again, without fear. But now I would observe very attentively all those I met. Didn't they too have a false soul? In the restaurants where I took my meals I would see lone and sad men, hunched over their plates. They were eating with difficulty, as if they had lost all their teeth. In the evenings, in the dim light of the restaurants, they seemed to be in despair, not to care anymore; and I recognised that several of them were shedding their souls like borrowed clothing that was too big for them. Was I like that too? They seemed unhappy. Only the children I met in the parks or sunny garden squares seemed happy. I would watch them running around, lithe and unfettered, for their souls were neither clogged nor replaced with false ones. But for how long will they be like this? If they have the ill luck to escape death in action they will wear out their souls, they will ruin them, and like me, and like so many others, will need a replacement.

It had become almost an obsession for me, but it seemed there were more and more people who were provided with a false soul, sometimes mounted on gold, sometimes mounted on rubber or on other more accessible materials. Was it the consequence of the wartime food shortage? Perhaps souls needed certain substances found in fruit and vegetables which were no longer available.

Souls became weaker, they even finally gave up the ghost. Rivalries, selfishness, had also become more bitter. Men no longer had any consideration for each other. Everyone was preoccupied with their own needs. All that caused suffering to their souls. Business was booming for the remover of souls.

IV

THE CONFESSION OF
THE FALSE SOUL

One evening while I was sitting on my bed before getting into it, I was reflecting on all the worries of the day which had just ended.

The bedroom was dark but to my surprise I realised that my shape was clearly visible in the mirror facing my bed. It was as if I was illuminated from within and I decided that there must be phosphorus in the mount supporting my soul. I saw myself then like a tree in the midst of which crouched the soul I had been given. From the mirror it looked into my eyes. It seemed uncomfortable and unhappy.

"You've never talked to me," I said to it then. "Talk to me. I'm your friend."

But it kept quiet, sullen.

"Do you think I'll listen to you less carefully than that collection of spiritualists before whom you almost exposed me did? Why are you sulking? It wasn't me who chose you to replace the soul which had been removed from me. Of course, you could have done better."

"I don't hold it against you," the poor soul eventually replied. "I know that the fate which has joined us together was none of your doing. But think a little bit about all that passionate youthfulness that I threw away in vain. As you already know, I'm the soul of a young soldier. I put my all into it, I was wounded, and what was it all for? So that in the end I should be nothing but a dull fixture in the breast of a low-level Finance Company employee. My joie de vivre, my enthusiasm, deserved something better. You drag me with you into that miserable office where all you do is wait for it to be time to eat or to go to bed. What do I have to look at as I crouch over your stooped body? The walls covered with memos and statistical charts. Are there any songs anywhere? A wonderful woman clad in all her beauty, her hands wandering amongst piano keys? Do people still put words together like stones which when rubbed together produce a spark which can light up the heavens? The soldier's life accustomed me to panoramic vistas, to changes of scenery, to surprise encounters. And now look at me, reduced to the prison of your mediocre carcass. It's enough to make me wonder if it was worth dying for."

I could only keep quiet on hearing this speech. What could I have said in response? It was true that nothing special had yet come of my life. A few inconclusive love affairs had left me sceptical, not knowing which way to turn. Love! That was the answer! It was no doubt love which haunted this soul, which had become a simple prosthesis so early in its life. I could see it crouching for ever inside my body. It had been worn down by long months inside me and now was less robust.

"Love! Talk to me about your love affairs as a young soldier."

"That dates back to before my military career really took off," the soul began. "I was only just a teenager when I met a lovely young girl. She was studying music and in the evenings I would often listen to her playing, with my elbows resting on her piano. We thought we would get married, once I had done my bit for the war. Amongst the smoke and acrid taste of an armoured vehicle I would often dream of the life we would lead together. Neither the noise of cannon fire nor the dreadful crashing of war machines could blot out her melodious voice. I saw myself holding her for hours in my arms. Alas, none of that ever came to pass."

And the soul was quiet again, plunged back into sadness.

"Come, my soul, give me some more details. From tomorrow I shall set about looking for her."

But I only received the vaguest hints in which the constant refrain was that she was a girl without equal, with snow-white hands, feet like mother-of-pearl and so on, all the qualities which a fervent lover usually attributes to the object of his desires. Nevertheless, I learned that she lived with her father, in the lower part of the town close to the sea. The soul spoke with difficulty, more like sighs, as if a wound had been opened up in it. From the snatches of its memories I managed to put together an image of a small house in the country, situated at the edge of town, with a jolly weathercock at the door, a small square courtyard with a well in the middle of it, barred windows through which a gentle light gleamed coming from small rooms with old-fashioned furniture. And the soul again was sinking into sadness.

"Sitting at her piano she was even more beautiful. Her face shone and one would have said the sounds came not from the instrument but from her own body. Have you ever seen a boat skimming rapidly over the sea? You get the impression that if the sea suddenly ceased to exist the boat would continue its journey, nimbly and joyfully, not stopping until the impression stops. In the same way, when she played, vibrant and taut like a flag flying high, I had the impression that if the piano were removed the music would continue to fall from her alluring hands and from her arms. Isn't that how where there used to be a forest you can still hear the wind murmuring in its branches and leaves? But the piano and the pianist have been swallowed up in the melancholy of a past time."

That was all my unfortunate soul told me in its lyrical outburst.

That night, for the first time since my own soul had been removed, I slept badly. Besides, I found it rather strange to have to suffer the pain and despair of a soul mounted on rubber. Was it worth the bother of removing my own soul only to find myself again having one that was gnawed, even eaten up, by nostalgia and regrets.

V

FIRST SEARCHES

The following day I decided I would try to find the pianist's peaceful home. Deep down, I said to myself, the roles can be reversed. It's not my body that has a false soul, it's the soul of that young man in love that is stuck in a false body, mine. And perhaps, with her lover's eyes, the beautiful musician will see in me the man she must marry.

Early in the morning therefore I set off towards the southern district of the town. It was previously the fishing port. But gradually, as this part was more exposed to the sun, large elegant beaches replaced the fisheries. The latter had emigrated towards the east and the west.

The town was perched on a peninsula surrounded on three sides by the sea. Alongside the magnificent private houses around here were the modest homes of retired people or workers who had left the town centre to live in the open air of the suburbs. The sea was sparkling in the luminous morning light and on it a few sail boats were setting off. I also noticed a few heavy fishing boats which had stayed there like a testimony to the richness of these fish-filled waters.

Some nicely dressed young women were hurrying towards the tram stops. They were shorthand typists, secretaries, dressmakers' assistants, salesgirls, children's maids hired by the day, making their way to work. Here and there a mother at the gate of her small garden would watch her daughter until a bend in the road had taken her out of sight. I stopped in front of doors, haphazardly. The sun was now brightly reflected off the pavement. Housewives were shaking sheets out of windows. Several times I heard piano chords ringing out.

They were small peaceful houses with balconies festooned with ivy and wisteria. My heart was moved to hear the scales. I remembered the quiet mornings of my happy childhood when my sister would practise the piano. I was in a light and airy bedroom, leafing through an album or a travel book with strange photos of Indians, aboriginals or Chinese.

I leaned with folded arms on the railings and for a long time listened keenly to the musical chords. It wasn't the first time I'd listened like this. I had always enjoyed stopping beneath a window behind which a life was being lived. I would imagine a room where the light was filtered through heavy curtains. An adolescent girl playing clear notes on a keyboard and as her hands and her eyes slide over the notes her thoughts stray into the distance towards a future of happiness. Her fiancé is a young medical student. They haven't yet revealed their love to their parents. The loving mother, like an invisible domestic god, is somewhere in the kitchen or the loft, busy with housekeeping work. The father, conscious of his duty, is in town doing an honest day's work. And in the room there floats an aroma of safety and wellbeing.

I turned my head which was swimming with this same dream. But I remembered in time that I didn't come here to indulge in my usual dreams but to seek my soul's companion.

I stood on tiptoe two or three times to look in through half-open windows. But all I saw were very young girls practising the piano or having lessons. These could not be the pianist I was looking for.

VI

THE BLACK HEN

Towards midday I came back to the seaside
promenade where, next to the tram stop, was
a group of small open-air restaurants. Here
there were people strolling around as they
waited until it was time for lunch. On a bench
in the full sun a large woman dressed in black
with her head wrapped in a scarf caught my
attention. Her dress, in a very old-fashioned
style, looked rather like a crinoline. Its folds
covered almost all of the bench and she had
to squeeze it hard to make a little room for
me. I could not stop looking at her face where
countless wrinkles were mixed with bright
colours, for the old woman was wearing make-

up. Her hooked nose and the fixed look in her eyes, which were sometimes covered by her white lashless eyelids, almost scared me. Then a large, heavy black hen appeared from under her dress. I was amused by the unexpectedness of this appearance. The hen was so fat it had difficulty moving; its legs were buckling under the weight of its shiny body. The old woman let out a cackle and the hen, turning towards her, seemed to respond. The resemblance between the old woman's face and the hen's amazed me. The woman's lips scarcely moved, and it was more from her throat and her nose, which so much resembled the hen's beak, that her words were coming, sounding like a hen's clucking. I could hear such expressions as "my girl" or "my darling", and especially *Krrrr* and *Kaw Kaw*, as well as diphthongs and strange vowel sounds. These unknown words seemed to have an excellent effect on the hen, which would respond with little cries of satisfaction. The sun was shining brightly between its black feathers. It swayed from side to side, as if it was being stroked. Now and again it would draw crosses and X's by rubbing its beak against the pavement. It made a dry sound like walnuts being cracked. I was still far from thinking that this was a witch taking the bird which helped her weave her evil spells out for air. The passers-by seemed to know her for, from time to time, some would speak to her.

"Hey, Aunt Marguerite, when are we going to eat her?"

"Isn't she fat enough for the soup yet, Aunt Marguerite?"

Then the old woman lowered her head and stayed quite still, with the worrying sidelong look of a hen listening to a mysterious and imperceptible noise.

I remembered some old stories: a woman practising witchcraft had managed to turn one of her rivals into a hen. And for years this hen assists her in her evil work. It needs a pure soul to come up to her and, recognising her beneath her fowl's appearance, to liberate her from her fate. And when the hen becomes a radiant woman again—for whilst the years have aged and wrinkled the sorceress they have had no such effect on the bewitched woman—all the power of the magician is gone.

Who knows how many other wizards around the world have transformed their enemies into donkeys, frogs, hens or other animals? Yet the power of wizards is easy to defeat. Suppose a pure spirit, a young spirit like the one I bore, presents itself to them and utters an anti-magic formula: mice escape from their cages and turn into good-natured boys. Snakes and bats become young men and young girls. What good has all the knowledge of these wizards done them? Here they are embarrassed and humbled before their victims, who have the right to judge them.

So whilst scholars devote their lives to researching the possibilities of adapting for humans with attractive characteristics the strong healthy souls of animals, here are wizards and magicians turning young men and women into animals. Suppose no pure soul comes to speak the anti-magic formulas in front of them: these beings risk coming to the end of their lives still inside the skins of donkeys, pigs, horses, or any other animal. They can have young ones who won't even know that one of their parents, or one of their ancestors, has been a man or a woman, condemned by the evil practices of a witch.

Thus, if there are on the earth men with the souls of animals (but thanks to the praiseworthy work of scholars), there are animals with the souls of men. Innumerable misfortunes lie in wait for the latter for they run the risk of being eaten by their own brothers, men, or being subjected to agonising labours, to a deprived and painful existence. For a mere pittance they can be made to suffer, for who would care about the condition of these poor beasts dragging heavy carts in the mines, or turning mill wheels, or labouring between factory conveyor belts? There is of course the Society for the Protection of Animals, which is preoccupied mainly with the welfare of dogs and cats, but its efforts are turning out to be inadequate. Perhaps the Society doesn't even realise that amongst these poor animals there are men like you and me. The shameful manoeuvrings of the witches have to stop. It will be necessary to start by confiscating their tools and equipment. The cauldrons where they boil their magic beverages could serve more noble purposes—war for example—they could be recycled along with other old metals. Their wands, their retorts, could be displayed as fine museum objects. But above all their broomsticks could be put to admirably good use to help relieve the crisis in means of transport which humanity has been suffering from for a while. As for them, they can go on foot to their witches' sabbaths. Their broomsticks would serve for public transport, or even, if more carefully adapted, would make a splendid private means of conveyance.

Already new horizons were opening up in front of the soul I bore. With its young and courageous soldier's purity I was going to rid the world of the power of wizards and witches. Those poor animals living a life of heavy toil from dawn until late at night would become cheerful men again.

I remember the day long ago in my childhood when a bee had come into my bedroom through a sunlit window. It buzzed around my head, seemed to want to land on my shoulder, but I was frightened and chased it away. It buzzed around a bit more near the window, and then flew quickly towards the garden. I watched it for a moment and suddenly on the path where it had vanished a beautiful young girl appeared. No doubt it was the bee whose human form I had unknowingly restored to it with a gesture. For witches don't always transform their victims into ugly and unfortunate beasts. Sometimes they amuse themselves by turning them into nice little canaries, or bees, or hens.

As if it had guessed the thoughts and quivering of my soul the black hen had come up to me. Chance had brought us together, me and the hen. "I'll start with her. But what is the formula I have to pronounce?" The old woman, suddenly alarmed, picked up the hen and stuffed it under her dress. I tried to remember the rhymes of childhood:

> *A hen on a shed*
> *Picking at dried bread*
> *Picky here, picky there*
> *Out will come the most fair*

. . . I murmured, but no miracle came to pass. I tried to remember more nursery rhymes and to aid my memory closed my eyes. When I opened them again a few moments later I was alone on the bench. I looked along the promenade and amongst the crowd I discerned the fat crinoline-clad stooping silhouette of the old woman walking along with a woman beside her. I tried to catch her up but she disappeared round a bend.

"The devil take the old thing," I cried and went to sit at a table in a modest restaurant.

When I had finished my meal I became more reasonable. "What hallucinations are these?" I asked myself. "Now I'm taking an honest inhabitant of these parts for a witch." And, more calm now, I decided not to be further distracted, and started my search again.

I was relying as much on chance to find the little house and the pianist as on the hope that a quiver from my false soul would help me to recognise them.

It was the beginning of Spring and the air was soft and fragrant. Windows were bright with geraniums and cyclamen. The sea, which could be glimpsed between the houses, was also calm and luminous. Urchins were singing in the courtyards. And suddenly I felt that I was at peace. Yes, peace had settled onto this part of the world. There was no more war, there were no more wandering souls, no more animals with human souls, no more men with animal souls, no more sadness, no more lies. In this peace, not only had armies laid down their arms but men, all men, nature itself, the whole universe, had broken away from their hatreds and their injustices and were now getting ready for a life of happiness and love. I felt that even inside me the false soul had had to make its peace with me.

VII

THE PHOTOGRAPHER

A fun-fair had been set up on a piece of waste ground nearby. Coming out of a small street I suddenly found myself in front of numerous booths where a happy crowd was milling around, laughing. Here, children and young men were testing their strength by pushing a small locomotive. By getting it up to the top of the rails the strongest of them succeeded in lighting a small lamp and making a bell ring. Over there, there was a carousel with ponies, goats, lambs and little cars pulled along by teams of angels. There was also the big wheel, panoramas, the magic lantern, freaks, snake-women, wall-of-death riders. A hubbub was enveloping me, drawing me in. In the midst of the young crowd I didn't notice that night had fallen. I had stopped in front of a photographer's little stall. Outside it, in a glass case, were displayed faded and blackened photographs in which housemaids in their Sunday best, soldiers, schoolchildren, smiled in their stiff poses.

"Come in, have your photo taken, it will make a nice souvenir," the photographer invited me from the door of his stall.

He was a small hunch-backed man. As he spoke he blinked his eyes and pulled faces, as if indicating to me that there were things he could not talk to me about in public. Besides the crowd was attracted by other pleasures and the stall seemed empty. A shooting gallery next to it kept the visitors back.

"Why not?" I replied to the photographer, thinking that since getting a false soul I had not yet had my photograph taken.

Once I was through the little door I found myself in a sort of large tent. The camera, from which hung a sleeve like a large black snake, was in the middle. The night which had fallen outside had not yet penetrated through these cloth walls. There reigned the gentle light of late afternoon. You would have said that the cloth had remained imprinted with the fading daylight.

"There, stand behind the car," the photographer said to me, indicating a large cardboard model of the side view of a limousine. "Would you prefer the boat?" he added when I hesitated, "or the balcony of this little house?"

I opted for the balcony.

"It won't take long," the photographer assured me. "Don't move. There we are! It's done!"

A few minutes later he took two still damp postcards out of a small cabin at the back of the tent and handed them to me. I glanced at them quickly. But what is the emotion gripping my heart? Here I am on the balcony of a small house like the one my soul had described to me in his confession. Yet the poster which had provided the setting was just a dismal expressionless drawing. Or perhaps I hadn't paid it enough attention. I was leaning over the balustrade. Ivy and wisteria reached up as far as my arms. The windows were open. But what is this (taking my breath away)! A young very beautiful girl is smiling next to me. Her hand is raised to touch my shoulder.

"I don't understand it at all," I said to the photographer. "I was alone when I posed for the photograph."

The poor man could not believe his eyes.

"It must be a superimposition. I didn't realise the plate had been used before."

And he babbled his apologies, assuring me he had just taken the plate from a packet that he hadn't opened for days. He proposed taking another photo. But for me, on the contrary, I was enchanted by the photo. And from the joy pounding in my breast I realised that the soul was also happy.

"I don't dislike the photo at all," I told the photographer. "But I do want to ask you something else: tell me, who is the young girl smiling next to me?"

The little hunchback held the photo up, went back into his stall, came out again looking worried and examining the black plate and finally said to me:

"I understand it less and less. The plate hadn't been used before. It's not a superimposition, as I'd thought to start with. Unless you or someone," (and he looked me up and down disapprovingly) "Unless you or someone has played a joke on me."

I paid and went outside where I mixed with the crowd. The lamps had been lit. There were fewer people, for most had gone home for their evening meal. I was clutching the two postcards in which the photographer had not only reflected my image but also the secret thoughts of my soul. I no longer had any doubt: the image of the young girl was that of the pianist I was seeking. And equally, the small house had thus appeared to me. Now I would be able to recognise it. It was in the photo, with its flower-covered balcony, with its shiny windows. So I couldn't complain about my first day's search.

Back at home there was a letter waiting for me from a friend inviting me to lunch the next day, which was a Sunday, in her house in the district to which I needed to return. I went to sleep happy, with the two photos under my pillow.

VIII

COD À LA MATRASSE

It was a Sunday such as I had not seen for a long time. Winter had passed very quickly, and I noticed that it was already the end of April.

"Today, my soul," I said to it, standing in front of the mirror, "we shall not be thinking about anything. We'll have a nice day in the suburbs at my friend's house. With her housekeeping talents she will have prepared a lovely meal despite the restrictions. We will get back to our search another time."

I got off the tram by the sea, from where I had a good fifteen minutes' walk uphill before arriving at my friend's house. The road was lined with pines and plane trees. Old men in their gardens dreamed in the sunshine.

My friend's house was exactly like the others all around. The garden was surrounded by a stone wall and in the middle was the circular border of a well. The contours of the house combined the simplicity of a country dwelling and the elegance of a town residence. As I was early, I went past the house without stopping. The path led up to the green walls of a castle. On all sides semi-town dwellers and semi-peasants were busy around hen houses. Hens scratched about for food in the grass. Coming from the top of the hill towards me was a child's baby car pushed by a little girl. I allowed the freshness of this Spring day to seep into me. The air carried the scent of the sea and the mountains. Close by were silhouetted the high stony hills. I retraced my steps and this time rang my hostess's doorbell. She opened the door smiling at me and babbling apologies:

"My God, I'm running late!"

"No, I'm the one who's early."

"It's the cod à la matrasse which has delayed me," she replied . . . "It's wartime rations. Ah! If only I could have welcomed you like in the good old days . . ."

And she disappeared into the kitchen.

In the dining room, which was more like a hallway with its beautiful wooden staircase in the middle—the house had a first floor where my young friend had a small apartment, the ground floor being reserved for her parents—I found the latter busy setting the table. A young airman, on leave from distant colonies, was already sitting alongside his young wife and two female cousins who were friends of the mistress of the house. And just then—for when I arrived he had been hanging up his overcoat in the hallway—a charming and whimsical friend whom I had not seen for a while and whom I was happy to rediscover had also taken his place.

"What have you been doing with yourself?" he cried.

And, watching me for a moment, he added:

"There's something different about you. Your spirit seems to be elsewhere."

My friend was an engineer endowed with a vast range of knowledge in many fields. Having spent time in the East he had come back with a deep understanding of the human soul. The musician, the artist and the poet in him yielded nothing to the mathematician. Amongst other things he had specialised in the culinary arts and, with a depth that surprised and amused you at the same time, he knew how to deduce from a simple dish the language, the history, the customs and the complete character of a country or a people.

I could hear the sound of live coals, and an odour of frying salty food came in through the open door between the kitchen and the dining room.

"Let's go and see how cod à la matrasse is prepared," said my friend.

And we went through into the kitchen where our hostess, with the help of her father, was removing the cod from the open fire. The airman, who had spent his childhood in that neighbourhood, was happy to rediscover a dish that he had liked. He started to crush some black olives and to cut up onions, mixing it all with oil and vinegar.

"Fortunately we still have a little oil, and we've just got our butter ration too," the father said to us.

Then, after giving the cod a shake because it still had some remnants of embers on it, he set about separating it on a plate. With the preparations finished we all took our places again around the table. In the middle of it, in the place of honour on a hot plate, was a small soup tureen holding the *bagna cauda*.

"You'll like this hot sauce," the hostess said to me. "It's made with anchovies and sautéed garlic in melted butter."

I did as the others did: I dipped the stem of raw celery into the tureen and I found the sauce exquisite.

Nothing could delight me more than this intimate and friendly atmosphere with each person dipping a piece of bread or vegetable into a communal pot. How I would have liked those moments to stretch out. I loved that peaceful life, this house where solitude's mournful breath could not penetrate. Why did I have to struggle with desires and sorrows, constantly mindful of my pain, of the world's pain? A table with relatives and friends gathered around it, a healthy and simple meal resonating like the chimes of a bell with the spirit of a country, what more could I wish for? But alas, I would soon be leaving that peaceful environment to return to the torment of my regrets and my researches.

Here, I joined in and broke with the others the white bread of laughter. But why was I just a passer-by?

That young and beautiful hostess could have been my wife or my sister.

IX

IN PRAISE OF GARLIC

I suddenly revealed that I was fond of garlic. So much so that the hostess added a little garlic to the cod à la matrasse just to please me.

"One day I would like to write a piece in praise of garlic."

"That would be a bold undertaking," said my friend pompously. "For garlic is in a sense the symbol of moderation, reserve and foresight. It looks self-effacing and modest and not even the strictest monastic order has a more sober and ascetic robe than garlic's. All is dry and brittle and before you get to its smooth and juicy flesh with its subtlety like that of a shelled almond you have to remove its covering of hard paper. Garlic is accumulated strength, silence, scorn for outward pomp and show. Like a candle it keeps watch in a room. It hates lies, that's why it's very rarely present at the banquets and feasts of the highly placed of this world. But the simple man, the brave labourer, the hunter, the poacher, the clever fisherman, the vagrant—they honour it. And when it has blessed a man's mouth with its generous fire it leaves around it a halo keeping enemies away. For garlic is a lucky charm, staving off ill fate and unlucky encounters. Only those who love you will come near you when you're giving off garlic's essence. It radiates, it makes waves in the air like a stone thrown into water, and its light spreads out in circles. Does it not resemble a dove's white throat? Don't plunge your knife into it. Pick it up honestly in your hand, openly, and if you want to remove its narrow portals rub it, roll it in your palm. Eat several cloves, without worrying about upsetting anyone. Its strong perfume will purify the air of all other perfumes. Open your houses to it, hang it from the beams, from your kitchen rafters. They are so touching, these long and tough strings of heads of garlic woven together. They adorn your home better than ribbons or the fairy lights of ballrooms. They are the moorings which attach it to the ground and which fight against the storm. And alongside the strings of garlic joyful little red and green pimentos glow, like pretty carnival crowns. And to complete the picture, hanging on long threads, like little bells with their dimpled cheeks, are dried mushrooms.

"Let the place of honour be given to garlic. It is the support and friend of the unlucky ones. When riches disappear, when the vagrant is alone with his humble bundle, when the emigrant deep in the ship's hold opens his violin case, the faithful garlic is still detectable. Perhaps it is the sign of a closed sect. Garlic's servants recognise and salute each other.

"Let's look together at this happy scene: a convoy of caravans is seeking somewhere to set up camp. For night has arrived like a thief amongst the horses and soon it will lead them along secret paths where no one will be able to see them anymore. Only their neighing will disturb the delicate starlight around their muzzles. And whilst the women, sheltered beneath tarpaulins, prepare the straw for a well-deserved sleep, the large and bearded men, like tanned kings, gather around the sacrificial lamb. In a hole below an improvised grill a fire has been lit. And now the lamb is being covered with branches and soil. It is like the bride hidden beneath veils who will not show herself until the hour of the nuptials. The gypsies gather and, holding the garlic like a monstrance, move on to the rites of the feast. The lamb will rise resuscitated and browned from the earthy womb. Nearby a group of young gypsies are using a stick to stir the maize polenta over a log fire in a large "tchéaoun"[1]. And when the round moon of the polenta is turned out onto a wooden board, the other

---

1 The vessel in which Turkish coffee is made.

moon, like a heavenly polenta, can be seen between the branches.

"At this feast the garlic is the Cinderella. It has thrown off its garments of torn paper and now appears in its limpid and regal nudity. Some children will go to the nearby stream to fetch fresh water which is the sole accompaniment loved by garlic. For garlic is so pure that it is troubled by any other drink than the crystal-clear water of the rocks. Now it spreads its blessing upon the lamb, upon the polenta, upon the "bourduf"[1] cheese. Praise be to the night which is heralded by garlic, when the air spins like a pigeon and falls into the clear carafe. A people of kings has risen to welcome the miraculous child. It comes up to the dying, puts its fingertip into their mouths and with its powerful breath restores them to life.

"Is it not the proof of its celestial predestination that high up where only pine trees dare to go the ozone-impregnated air has its

---

1 A type of Romanian ewe's milk cheese.

perfume? Perhaps the whole universe is but an enormous head of garlic, the planets its cloves. And the long tails of the comets are just its odour wafting in the air. Those who refuse garlic here will be banished from the stars elsewhere. It is the earth's body itself that I'm sharing. Take this, it is the flesh of the universe."

My friend's enthusiastic praise and his reference to the virtue of water did not stop the hostess's father coming up from the cellar with a vintage wine. We celebrated this reunion, the togetherness of family and friends.

"It's just a wartime meal," the lovely hostess repeated.

And for dessert she served a pumpkin and prune tart.

"You're a magician," we all exclaimed, for the tart was a great success.

"I'm not the magic one, our friend is," and she looked affectionately at the engineer. "He's the one who gave me the recipe for this tart."

And he himself, with his face alight, was leaning now towards one, now towards another, discussing a thousand profound matters in a light and playful tone.

I was slightly embarrassed, for with his penetrating look he could have noticed that I had a false soul. The airman, who had cigarettes, offered them round. We lit them and then listened to him as he told us stories of the war, mixed with stories of strange meals.

"I've eaten everything," he said, laughing. "One day, in New Caledonia, I ate in the same meal a small Chinese dog, a snake steak, swallows' nest soup and cabbage palm worms."

He certainly had his own soul, that man. He wasn't afraid to talk loudly, to hold the glance of those listening to him. Conscious of his authentic soul he did not hesitate to return to the battlefield. The poor man, he didn't know that one day his soul would serve as covering for a worn-out body, as a stand-in for a lost soul.

X

VISIT TO A NEIGHBOUR'S

"I've a surprise for you," our young hostess said to us when she'd served the coffee. "An old friend of my family who lives next door has invited us all to spend the afternoon there."

We accepted with enthusiasm and there we were at the gate of the little garden. The house was like that of our hostess. The same well, the same ivy, in the courtyard the same table with its legs made from tree branches, the same windows, the same balcony. Looking at the balcony I remembered the photograph. The same balcony! . . . Perhaps that is why a profound emotion gripped me as soon as I entered the hallway. In the corner of the hall, which corresponded to the dining room of our hostess, there was a grand piano.

The old lady greeted us kindly. She was of medium height, wearing a dress rather like a kimono, and her white hair was partly covered with a brightly-coloured headscarf. The house was full of statuettes, screens, cushions, fans with Chinese patterns, but although all these objects were piled up on one another they did not create an impression of clutter. There was a lightness here, and even our voices and laughter were slightly subdued, as if we were in the far distance and our words were nothing but an echo of themselves. We sat down around a table and the old lady served us a rose sorbet, as was the custom in I know not which country.

Straight away, we talked about the difficulties in obtaining all sorts of things, like the sugar in this sorbet which the old lady assured us she had received from friends living in far away countries. The sorbet shimmered in small spoons at the bottom of glasses of water. The pure water from the bottom of the well was shared between us from the carafe. Afterwards there was coffee, served in small cups of an Arabic design.

"I had quite a problem getting my old things into this small house."

And the lady explained to us what our friend had omitted to tell us, that the house we were in had belonged to one of the lady's brothers. The brother's only daughter had volunteered as a nurse and had perished on a ship making its way to the colonies.

"She was a real musician," added the lady. "And this is her piano. I have tried to find the inspiration at the keyboard which fired my niece, but even though in this house I feel under the spell of music, I have not succeeded."

"Play us something," we all begged her.

XI

THE WOMAN FOUND AND LOST AGAIN

I had approached the beautiful instrument on the dark wood of which the light's reflections gleamed like previous stones. On the piano a small photo with its black frame drew my attention.

"I know that face!" I could not help exclaiming.

"You knew my niece?" the old lady asked me.

"It's too difficult to explain," I replied, as under the astonished gaze of my friends I compared the face of the young woman standing next to me in the photo from the fair with that of the pianist.

Was I in the house of my poor soul's fiancée?

The old lady began to play and more than ever I felt in my breast the weight of this alien soul. The features and the story of this tragic figure were coming together to make sense. And I was hardly surprised that chance had brought me here. How could I have avoided this encounter? My life was mapped out for me by my soul. It was no coincidence. It was the destiny that my soul was forging for me.

Ah! God of men and nature, did you want me to learn at the same moment of the real existence and the death of the woman I would have loved with the purest love? With the love of my soul.

"It was her favourite piece," said the lady, starting to play a rhapsody by Liszt.

The outpourings of music, like swirls of dust on a road, came and went, fleeing from us then wrapping us in their virtual veils only to flee and return once again. We all listened in silence. The face of the old lady was transformed: she sat straight in her chair with only her shoulders rising and falling like the waves of the ocean, and her arms, like snakes, were in thrall to the chords. I gripped the back of an armchair to stop me from falling.

"What's going on?" the engineer asked me in his magician's tones.

And, taking my arm, he more or less dragged me to the garden. Once there, tears were running down my face.

"How can one suffer so much for someone else?" I exclaimed.

"For who else?"

Ah! Could I reveal my secret to him? My soul was beating inside me, it wished to be free and perhaps to go after the woman it loved with its deathly passion. I felt that my life had disintegrated. How could I still seem so proud and brave when my soul was so tormented.

"Let's go back in," I said to my friend, for in no way did I wish to get myself noticed.

The pianist had stopped playing. She was showing my friends a medallion inside which, she said, a charm was hidden, an amulet which she had brought back from a journey to Singapore.

"This little bag has to stay with me all the time; it will come with me even to the grave. There is a pact between this amulet and my soul. I had sent a similar one to my niece who was no doubt wearing it when she was shipwrecked."

I took advantage of a moment when my friend was looking elsewhere to slip outside the little house again, this time alone. I went towards the sea. Turning my head, I noticed that my friend had followed me. Since it was at sea that the beloved had perished, I just had to throw my soul into the sea. The beloved woman and the soul would thus finally find each other again in the quivering eternity of the waves. Moreover, is not the sea a giant piano? Down at the bottom are the strings, made to reverberate by the black or white keys of the fish. The wonderful young woman must give some magnificent concerts down there. And I pressed on, hoping to escape the watchfulness of my friend. Once at the water I removed my jacket and hat and without worrying about the rest of my clothes I entered the waves. Once under I wanted to remove my soul, carry it as far as possible out to sea, and then come back to dry land. But I had not counted on my friend's perseverance.

"What are you doing, wretched man?" he shouted to me, swimming strongly towards me.

He finally got hold of me and dragged me towards the bank. I had had just enough time to get rid of the false soul.

I was now stretched out on the sand. My friend was speaking gently to me.

"Why did you want to kill yourself?" he was saying to me. "Have you given up on the projects you were planning as recently as yesterday for releasing the poor human beings transformed by wizards into animals?"

"What," I cried, amazed, "you knew that was what I was planning?"

And in my friend's eyes there was the shining light of a magician who misses nothing. Of a kind magician, for there are also magicians who are ready to bring joy to the wretched. And my friend was one of those. But how should I explain to him that, far from wishing to commit suicide, all I had wanted to do was restore my poor artificial soul to the woman it adored. It was all the same to me now: whether men were beasts or not was of little consequence to me. I felt light and empty. The salt water I had swallowed as I struggled had washed out of me the last traces of the soul.

In the distance I could see a white haze over the water. I nodded to it, for I realised that it was the soul, floating happily amidst the foam. Like a pillar of salt the soul was floating between sky and sea. It must already have found its heart's delight. Freed from my earthly shackles it could finally sing its love song amongst the storms and stars. My body could just return to its trivial business as an employee, head accountant, supervisor, director, or even, who knows, chairman of the board. You could do all that without a soul. Even without a substitute soul.

Deep in one of my wet pockets I found the two postcards from the fair. They were crumpled and soaked. And, strange to relate, only my own image remained on the photos. The sea water had wiped away the pianist's face. The house and balcony too were blurred and unrecognisable. And yet the photographer himself had seen the young woman's form appearing at my side. So the vision of its tragic love had departed along with my soul.

"You'd do better to get rid of those photos," my friend said to me, in a tone which implied that he knew what he was talking about.

I stood up and threw the two postcards into the sea. Foam covered them straight away.

"Leave me now," I begged my friend, and with heavy footsteps I set off towards the town.

XII

A SOUL TO ORDER

And yet, as early as the following morning, I said to myself: why not order a new one? If I pay more perhaps I'll get a more comfortable soul. Besides, I had valid reasons for wanting a new soul. The Company where I worked had led me to hope that I would soon be upgraded and promoted. An important position had become vacant in the colonies. I would have to be receiving eminent people, taking part in conferences or business lunches. You always make a better impression if you can show you have a soul.

But this time I had made a decision. I did not want another young soul, that of a passionate soldier, of someone disappointed with life. I was ready to give up all my regrets, my vague desires, but without taking the risk of suffering from the passions and anxieties of another soul. A career was definitely opening up in front of me. The end of miserable hours spent amongst dusty files. The end of simple meals in modest restaurants. I needed a soul without weakness and without melancholy. One day soon I would be the Director, the Head of a workforce which I'd have to manage without flinching. So I absolutely needed a strong soul, an animal's soul. If bulls, calves and pigs were too scarce, if donkeys had long since disappeared, sacrificed to make the drums which sounded the attack during military manoeuvres, there was still a way of organising a hunt to satisfy the requirements of a personality as talented as mine. The Director of a Limited Company may well have the soul of a boar or a wolf. If necessary I can wait until the cold spells when the wolves come and prowl around close to the towns.

As for my idea about one day taking on the magicians and witches and giving back a happy life to animals with human souls, there could no longer be any question of that. Such ideas were fine for a low-level employee with no future. But such trifles should not concern the future Director I was now revealed to be. The only thing I was interested in was to have a soul capable of helping me to make my fortune as soon as possible.

So the very next morning I set off to see the surgeon. I had never been back there since my operation. I easily recognised the street. But once in front of the building I was astonished to find the walls smoke-blackened and falling into ruin. A half staved-in door opened onto a narrow dark staircase. A windblown poster proclaimed the surgeon's merits. The street, along with the houses on both sides, appeared worn out and sad. Everywhere a stifling smell of ashes and burnt dung prevailed. Suddenly the sound of a horse's hooves and the tinkling of a cab's bells brought me a vision of the far-off landscape of my childhood village. Horses were coming down the street in a haze of mist past my wondering gaze. I finally went over the threshold into the house and with my hand on the rickety bannister set off up the stairs. My legs felt heavy and I was short of breath. Would this staircase never end? On each step I had to avoid the holes ready to snatch my feet. Everything here was falling into ruin. It all smelled rotten, musty. At the top, a small paraffin lamp quivered in the darkness. At last, exhausted, only just able to drag myself along, I arrived at a flight of stairs hanging above the street. Desperately I clung to a windowsill, for there was no door on the side of the wall. On the other side, empty space. From inside, an old woman in a nurse's smock was looking at me, unsurprised, as if there was nothing more natural than to see me arriving there. I begged her to come to my aid, and she helped me to climb in through the window.

"You can see what a state I'm in," I whispered. "I need a soul."

It was then, looking closely at her, that I recognised her: the old woman was none other than the witch with the hen. Beneath her nurse's smock her crinoline was visible.

"A soul?" cried the nurse, bending over a register and leafing hastily though it. "But you've already had one," she said, as her finger stopped above a name which must have been mine. "What did you do with it?"

And her pitiless look had me trembling in fear.

"Well, follow me," she ordered, and she walked along a dark corridor in front of me.

Along the walls familiar-looking figures appeared for a moment before mingling immediately afterwards with the smoke. I thought I recognised my mother's face, but I knew I was mistaken for my mother had been dead for a long time. A young woman held out her arms to me, but I didn't stop and I continued to follow the old nurse. At last we arrived in the waiting room, where I collapsed, exhausted, into an armchair.

The air was still very heavy and I was having difficulty breathing. Moreover I had a strange feeling of not really being there. "All these things, all these beings I'm meeting, won't make me believe I'm really here." And this gave me courage (for, despite the dizziness and the anguish, I was still completely lucid). "What do I have to fear, deep down? Nothing can happen to me, for I'm somewhere else." And through a strange disconnection I could see myself, pale and dishevelled in the armchair, and I was aware that someone who might have been me could hear the voice of the surgeon through the half-open door: "Don't be afraid, you won't suffer." Someone who might have been me (and I smiled at this doubt) could hear the voice of an old gentleman with dyed hair telling his neighbours: "Yes, it was in Avignon that I bought this umbrella. Camboulives had an umbrella shop on the corner of the rue des Marchands and the rue Neuve. The maid was nothing but a thief. That was all before the previous peace."

A PARTIAL LIST OF SNUGGLY BOOKS